Happy Birthday, Buddy Blue

by Lyn Calder

A GOLDEN BOOK • NEW YORK
Western Publishing Company, Inc.
Racine, Wisconsin 53404

If you could travel to the very end of the rainbow, you
would find yourself in a wonderful place called
Rainbow Land.

Rainbow Land is the home of Rainbow Brite, a lovable little girl who brings joy and happiness to everyone by coloring the world. A handful of Star Sprinkles is all she needs.

Now, if you could get to Rainbow Land right away, maybe—just maybe—you would be invited to Buddy Blue's surprise birthday party.

"Bend and stretch! Bend and stretch! Jump...2...3...4!
Jump...2...3...4!" called Buddy Blue as he exercised
with Patty O'Green.

"Come on, Buddy," moaned Patty. "I'm tired already,
and we haven't even started to run."

"You have to warm up before you run," said Buddy. "Patty O'Green, you promised to come with me!"

"I will. I will," said Patty, remembering that it was her job to keep Buddy away from the Color Castle while it was being decorated for his surprise birthday party.

So Patty and Buddy finished their warm-ups. Meanwhile, the sprites and all the other Color Kids were working hard to get ready for Buddy's party.

The sprites were busy scrubbing the Color Castle from top to bottom. Twink, Rainbow Brite's favorite sprite, was hurrying them along.

10,000 BALLOONS

The Color Kids were filling the castle with star decorations and balloons of every color.

"You'd better be careful, Red Butler," said Rainbow Brite. "I don't think you should blow that balloon up much more..."

POP! It was too late. Everyone laughed at the look of surprise on Red Butler's face.

LaLa Orange ran to his side. "Are you all right?" she asked.

"Sure," said Red. "Just get me another balloon!"

By now, Buddy Blue and Patty O'Green had started on their run around Rainbow Land. Up to Red Region, down to Orange Meadows, through Yellow Plains, and straight into Green Grange.

Patty O'Green was huffing and puffing.

"I think it's time to rest," she said breathlessly, sitting down in a bed of green clover.

"I'll just take a quick spin around Blue Zone," called Buddy over his shoulder. "I'll be back to get you in no time."

As soon as Patty O'Green caught her breath, she began looking for a four-leaf clover. "That would make a fine birthday present for Buddy," she said to herself.

On a gray and gloomy hill just above Rainbow Land is a place called The Pits, where Murky Dismal and his helper, Lurky, live. Every day, Murky tries his hardest to make everyone as miserable as he is.

"Ah," said Murky Dismal, looking over Lurky's shoulder as he mixed a brew in a great pot. "Our doom potion is just about ready. Why don't we go try it out on one of those cheerful little Color Kids."

Murky.Dismal and Lurky packed up the potion and
climbed into their Grunge Buggy. They headed toward
Rainbow Land—straight toward the Blue Zone.

"I did it! I found one!" shouted Patty O'Green,
holding up a four-leaf clover. She started humming
"Happy Birthday to You."

"But where is Buddy?" she wondered. "He was going
to take a quick spin and then come back to get me." She
knew there was only one thing that would stop him
from coming back—Murky Dismal!

"I hope you're as lucky as you're supposed to be!" said Patty O'Green to her four-leaf clover. And she ran as fast as she could back to the Color Castle.

When she got there, she had to shout over the noise
of the Color Kids and the sprites.
"Buddy Blue is in trouble!" she said. "He went
jogging up toward the Blue Zone and never came back!"
"Oh, no!" said Rainbow Brite. "We've got to
help him!"

Rainbow Brite ran outside and began to call for Starlite, her magical flying horse. He had been sent out to look for flowers for the party. Starlite was admiring himself in the reflection of a pond. But when he heard Rainbow's call, he took off immediately for the Color Castle.

In a flash, he was at Rainbow's side.

"We've got to find Buddy Blue," she said. "He's in trouble. Quick, Starlite."

With Rainbow Brite on his back, Starlite flew over Rainbow Land toward the Blue Zone.

It wasn't long before Rainbow and
Starlite saw what they had feared. The
Grunge Buggy, with its gray cloud of
doom, was closing in on Buddy Blue.
Murky Dismal had his evil potion ready.
    Starlite swept down close and
Rainbow Brite cast out her magic color
crystals. As soon as they hit the potion,
a beautiful haze of color appeared.

"Oh, no!" cried Murky Dismal. "Faster, Lurky, faster!"

But Rainbow Brite's Star Sprinkles were already working their magic on Lurky.

"What's the hurry?" he said. "It's such a nice day for a buggy ride."

"Faster, you dimwit!" yelled Murky. "Don't let that kid get away!"

But it was too late. Buddy Blue climbed onto
Starlite's back behind Rainbow Brite.
"That was a close call," said Buddy. "Let's get out
of here!"

At the Color Castle, Patty O'Green was the first to see Rainbow, Starlite, and Buddy Blue coming. "Hurry!" she called. "They're almost here!"
Everyone ran to hide.

"Gee," said Buddy when they landed. "It's awfully quiet…"

"Happy Birthday!" shouted all his friends as soon as Buddy opened the castle door.

Twink came out carrying a star-shaped birthday cake. Buddy Blue made a birthday wish and blew out the candles. "Thank you, everyone," he said.

Patty O'Green handed Buddy the four-leaf clover.
"Here is a birthday present, Buddy. I think it brought
you luck today!"

Then Rainbow Brite took out a handful of Star
Sprinkles she saved for special occasions. When she
tossed them at Buddy, the air all around him lit up with
every color of the rainbow.
"Happy Birthday, Buddy Blue!" said Rainbow Brite.
And it was a birthday Buddy Blue would never forget.